First published in Great Britain 1986 by
Hamish Hamilton Children's Books
Garden House, 57–59 Long Acre, London WC2E 9JZ
Copyright © 1986 by Nigel Snell

British Library Cataloguing in Publication Data

Snell, Nigel
What do you say –?
I. Title
823′.914[J]   PZ7

ISBN 0–241–11814–X

Typeset by Kalligraphics Ltd, Redhill
Printed in Great Britain by
Cambus Litho, East Kilbride

Nigel Snell

WHAT DO YOU SAY..?

a child's guide
to manners

Hamish Hamilton · London

Always hold open the door for someone behind you.

Never get cross if a friend
breaks one of your toys
by mistake.

Don't take the biggest
piece of cake on
the plate.

Never talk with your mouth full, and always eat with your mouth closed.

Never wave your knife and fork about. You may hurt someone.

Always say thank-you
when you are given a
present.

Don't leave the table
until everyone has
finished eating.

Don't ride your bicycle through puddles and splash people.

Don't point at other people, or whisper behind their back.

On a bus or train always give up your seat to older people.

Always wave and say thank-you when a car or lorry stops for you at a zebra crossing.

Don't drop litter in the town or in the country.